Mouse of the Year

Based on the stories by Katharine Holabird
Based on the illustrations by Helen Craig

Grosset & Dunlap

Library of Congress Control Number: 2006024527

ISBN 978-0-448-44474-1   10 9 8 7 6 5 4 3 2 1

Angelina and Alice were buying candy at Mrs. Thimble's General Store when a pile of leaflets fell from the counter onto the floor.

"What's this?" asked Angelina, picking some up. "Mouseland's Teacher of the Year Award?"

"*This award honors the teacher who has shown
the highest level of dedication to her students,*" read
Angelina. "Oh, Alice! We must enter Miss Lilly.
Nobody deserves this award more than she does!"

That evening, Angelina and Alice sat down to make Miss Lilly's entry for the award. Angelina wrote a long letter while Alice put together a scrapbook.

"What are you writing, Angelina?" Alice asked.

"Well, that she makes us *all* feel special, like we're each the prima ballerina."

"Oh, yes," said Alice. "And she's always there when we need her, especially if we hurt ourselves or feel upset."

"I'll add that, too," said Angelina, scribbling away.

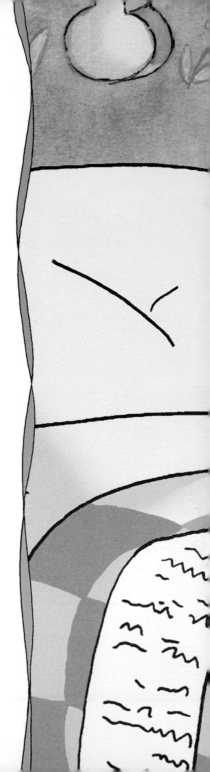

The following day at ballet class, Angelina brought the
letter for each of her classmates to sign. She had to be extra
careful that Miss Lilly didn't see what they were up to.

"Angelina? William?" asked Miss Lilly from the front of
the class. "What are you two doing over there?"

"Nothing, Miss Lilly!" they chimed as Angelina hid the
letter behind her back.

The letter and the scrapbook made a gigantic package. Angelina and Alice tried to stuff it in the mailbox, but it just wouldn't fit.

"We have to get it in, Alice!" said Angelina. "Today's the last day we can enter Miss Lilly in the contest!"

The two little mouselings pushed as hard as they could, and with one final nudge, they finally squeezed the package into the slot.

A few weeks later, Angelina and her classmates were practicing for their upcoming performance of *Sleeping Beauty*. Angelina was Sleeping Beauty, and William was the handsome prince.

"Now," said Miss Lilly, "the prince gently kisses Sleeping Beauty."

"Oh, crumbs," muttered William under his breath. He bent forward and kissed Angelina on the forehead as the rest of the class giggled.

Then there was a knock at the door. The
postmouse peeked his head into the classroom.

"Special delivery for you, Miss Lilly," he said.

"Oh, Miss Lilly!" cried Angelina. "Look at all the
gold and the fancy writing. It must be something very
important and special, and you really should look at
it right away!"

"All right, Angelina," said Miss Lilly, smiling as she
opened the letter.

She began to read: *"We are delighted to tell you that you have won the award for Teacher of the Year . . ."*

"Hooray!" interrupted all the mouselings. Angelina hugged Miss Lilly.

"It says here that I have to give a speech at the award ceremony next week," said Miss Lilly. "And that you have to give a speech, too, Angelina. Was this whole thing your idea?"

"It was Angelina's idea, but we all helped," said Alice.

"Well, thank you all so very much," Miss Lilly said.

Mr. Mouseling was taking a picture of Miss Lilly with Angelina for the *Mouseland Gazette*. "Smile!" he said.

But just as he snapped the photo, a fly buzzed by. "Oh!" cried Angelina as Miss Lilly swatted at the fly.

"That'll do for the paper, now, won't it, Mr. Mouseling?" said Miss Lilly.

"Err, yes, of course, Miss Lilly. Now let's go inside for the interview."

"All right," said Miss Lilly. "Angelina, please tell the class that I must cancel today's practice. We can catch up tomorrow."

The next day before ballet class, Angelina brought
the *Mouseland Gazette* to class. "My dad says there's a
picture of Miss Lilly and me in the paper today," she
told the mouselings.

"Oh, really?" said William.

"I want to see!" said Alice.

Angelina unfolded the newspaper. "You've been practically cut out!" exclaimed Alice.

"It does rather ruin the picture," snickered Penelope.

"Seeing you at all, that is!" Priscilla said, laughing.

Angelina ignored them, rolling her eyes. Then there was a loud creak as the door opened. "Miss Lilly!" Angelina cried.

But it wasn't Miss Lilly—it was Miss Quaver!

"All right, class," Miss Quaver announced. "Shall
we begin?"

"But where's Miss Lilly?" asked Angelina.

"She's out of town at a big dinner," Miss Quaver
said matter-of-factly. "She's guest of honor. And, um,
well, *I* am taking the class today."

"Oh, dear," muttered Angelina as Miss Quaver
turned toward the piano and began to play.

"She didn't even wait for us to get into our positions!" Alice whispered to Angelina as they rushed to catch up.

"To the left, Penelope!" called Miss Quaver, looking over her shoulder. "No, no! The *other* left!" she said as Penelope bumped right into Priscilla.

Meanwhile, William was doing a pirouette—but it looked like he couldn't stop turning! His face was beginning to look green.

"Um, Miss Quaver?" Alice piped up. "William is, um . . . oh!" she cried as a dizzy William fell to the floor.

Angelina sighed. *I hope Miss Lilly comes back soon,* she thought.

Angelina was so excited when Miss Lilly finally came back to town that she went to meet her at the train station.

"I had no idea being Teacher of the Year would be so exhausting," Miss Lilly told Angelina. "How were things with Miss Quaver?"

"Well, erm . . ." began Angelina. "They were, um, just fine."

"Maybe you don't need me anymore," Miss Lilly said, sighing.

"Oh, no, Miss Lilly!" Angelina cried. "We really missed you!"

Back in class, the mouselings were practicing their *Sleeping Beauty* routine. At the end, William kissed Angelina, finishing with a leap and a triumphant flourish.

"Ta-da!" said Angelina.

But there was no response from Miss Lilly. She had fallen asleep!

"Guess we'd better go," whispered William, and the class quietly left the room.

On the way out, Angelina angrily thumped her hand on the piano keys, making a very loud noise. Miss Lilly's eyes fluttered open, but then she fell right back to sleep.

"She probably just needs rest, Angelina," Alice said soothingly.

"Well, *we* need to practice!" countered Angelina.

Later, Angelina and Alice were getting ice cream from Mrs. Thimble's shop when they saw Miss Lilly and Miss Quaver passing by. Angelina and Alice huddled in the doorway to listen.

"I'm running all over Mouseland, and then I have to teach dance class," said Miss Lilly. "I can't do it all. I'll have to tell them."

"Tell us what?" Angelina asked Alice. "I'll bet she's giving up teaching us."

Alice frowned. "I'm sure she didn't mean . . ."

But Angelina interrupted her. "I wish I'd never entered her for that award!" she exclaimed. "And I'm going to say so in my speech tomorrow."

"Angelina, you can't!" said Alice.

"We'll see about that," Angelina said, crossing her arms.

The night of the award ceremony had finally arrived. Angelina was backstage getting ready to give her speech when Miss Lilly walked up beside her.

"Angelina," said Miss Lilly gently, "I need to speak to you."

"I know all about it!" Angelina said angrily. "I know you've been busy since you won this award, but I can't believe you'd give up teaching us!" Angelina exclaimed.

"Oh, Angelina!" said Miss Lilly, looking surprised. "I could never give up teaching. I wanted to tell you that I've decided to turn down this silly award."

Before Angelina could respond, there was a burst of applause from the theater. It was time for her speech!

Angelina walked onstage and stood nervously behind the podium, her knees shaking. She crumpled the speech she had written in her hand.

"I . . . I wanted Miss Lilly to win this award," she began as tears welled up in her eyes, "because I knew she was the best teacher in all of Mouseland. And now I know she's the best teacher in the whole world."

The audience cheered and clapped. Alice and William gave a standing ovation.

Just then, Miss Lilly came onstage to join Angelina. "Thank you, Angelina," she said proudly, hugging her.

The next day, Angelina and the other mouselings were gathered around the *Mouseland Gazette*.

"Teacher Chooses Mouselings over Prestigious Award," Angelina read the headline. *"Chipping Cheddar was shocked when their prize-winning Teacher of the Year turned down her award in order to spend more time with her pupils."*

"What's 'prestigious' mean?" asked Henry.

"It means *very* important," said Angelina.

Just then, Alice caught a glimpse of the photograph in the paper. "Angelina, you look just lovely!"

Priscilla leaned over Angelina's shoulder. "Er, what happened to us, Penelope?"

"You must be hidden behind Miss Lilly," said Alice, pointing.

"Ah, yes," said William. "And if you look *really* closely, I think that's Penelope's elbow in my ribs."

The mouselings all giggled. And Angelina smiled. She was glad to have her teacher back, just the way she was before.